THE

JONES LIBRARY

INCORPORATED

————

AMHERST, MASSACHUSETTS

WITHDRAWN

WITHD

D1295843

THE
FOUR LITTLE CHILDREN
WHO WENT
AROUND THE WORLD

by EDWARD LEAR
Pictures by Arnold Lobel

The Macmillan Company, New York · Collier-Macmillan Limited, London

J
L

COPY 3 ·S. A·
(ALL)

COPYRIGHT © ARNOLD LOBEL 1968

All rights reserved. No copyrighted component part of this book may be reproduced or transmitted in any form or by any means, electronic or mechanical, including photocopying, recording or by any information storage and retrieval system, without permission in writing from the Publisher.

The Macmillan Company, New York
Collier-Macmillan Canada, Ltd., Toronto, Ontario
Library of Congress catalog card number: 68-10068
Printed in the United States of America

FIRST PRINTING

THE FOUR LITTLE CHILDREN
WHO WENT AROUND THE WORLD

Once upon a time, a long while ago, there were four little people whose names were Violet, Slingsby, Guy and Lionel; and they all thought they should like to see the world.

1

So they bought a large boat to sail quite round the world by
sea, and then they were to come back on the other side by
land. The boat was painted blue with green spots and the
sail was yellow with red stripes: and when they set off they
took only a small Cat to steer and look after the boat, besides
an elderly Quangle-Wangle, who had to cook the dinner and
make the tea; for which purposes they took a large kettle.

2

For the first ten days they sailed on beautifully and found plenty to eat, as there were lots of fish; and they had only to take them out of the sea with a long spoon, when the Quangle-Wangle instantly cooked them; and the Pussy Cat was fed with the bones, with which she expressed herself pleased, on the whole: so that all the party were very happy.

During the daytime, Violet chiefly occupied herself in putting salt water into a churn while her three brothers churned it violently in the hope that it would turn into butter, which it seldom if ever did; and in the evening they all retired into the teakettle, where they all managed to sleep very comfortably while Pussy and the Quangle-Wangle managed the boat.

After a time they saw some land at a distance; and when they came to it they found it was an island made of water quite surrounded by earth. Besides that it was bordered by evanescent isthmuses, with a great gulf stream running about all over it, so that it was perfectly beautiful and contained only a single tree, 503 feet high.

4

When they had landed they
walked about but found to their
great surprise that the island was
quite full of veal cutlets and
chocolate drops and nothing else.
So they all climbed up the single high
tree to discover, if possible, if there
were any people, but having remained
on the top of the tree for a week and
not seeing anybody they naturally
concluded that there were no
inhabitants; and accordingly, when
they came down, they loaded the boat
with two thousand veal cutlets
and a million of chocolate drops;
and these afforded them sustenance
for more than a month, during
which time they pursued their voyage
with the utmost delight and apathy.

After this they came to a shore where there were no less than sixty-five great red parrots with blue tails sitting on a rail all of a row and all fast asleep. And I am sorry to say that the Pussy Cat and the Quangle-Wangle crept softly and bit off the tail feathers of all the sixty-five parrots, for which Violet reproved them both severely.

Notwithstanding which, she proceeded to insert all the feathers—two hundred and sixty in number—in her bonnet; thereby causing it to have a lovely and glittering appearance, highly prepossessing and efficacious.

The next thing that happened to them was in a narrow part of the sea which was so entirely full of fishes that the boat could go on no farther, so they remained there about six weeks till they had eaten nearly all the fishes, which were soles, and all ready-cooked, and covered with shrimp sauce, so that there was no trouble whatever. And as the few fishes who remained uneaten complained of the cold, as well as the difficulty they had in getting any sleep on

10

account of the extreme noise made by the arctic bears and the tropical turnspits, which frequented the neighborhood in great numbers, Violet most amiably knitted a small woolen frock for several of the fishes and Slingsby administered some drops to them; through which kindness they became quite warm and slept soundly.

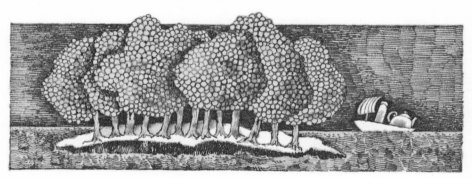

Then they came to a country which was wholly covered with immense orange trees of a vast size and quite full of fruit. So they all landed, taking with them the teakettle, intending to gather some of the oranges and place them in it. But while they were busy about this a most dreadfully high wind rose and blew out most of the parrot tail feathers from Violet's bonnet. That, however, was nothing compared with the calamity of the oranges falling down on their heads by millions and millions, which thumped and bumped and bumped and thumped them all so seriously that they were obliged to run as hard as they could for their lives, besides that the sound of the oranges rattling on the teakettle was of the most fearful and amazing nature.

11

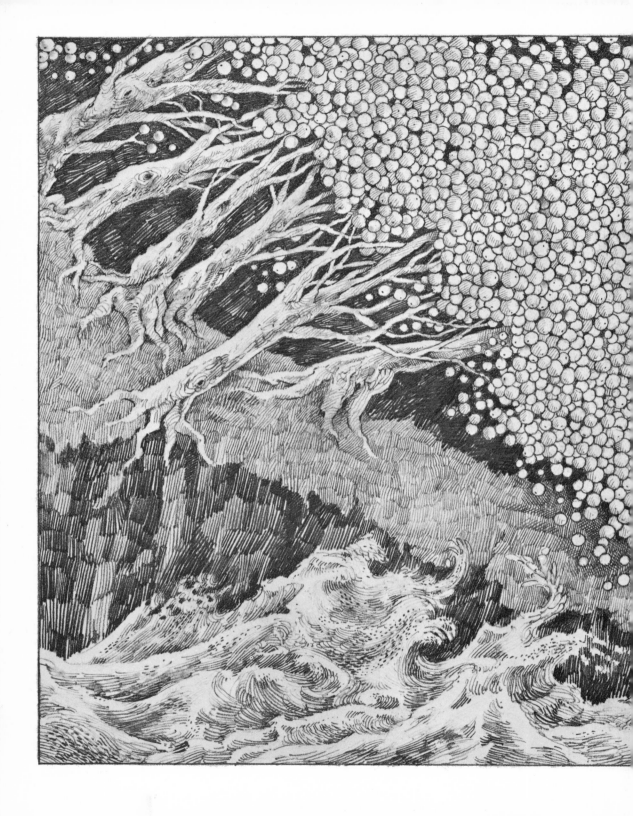

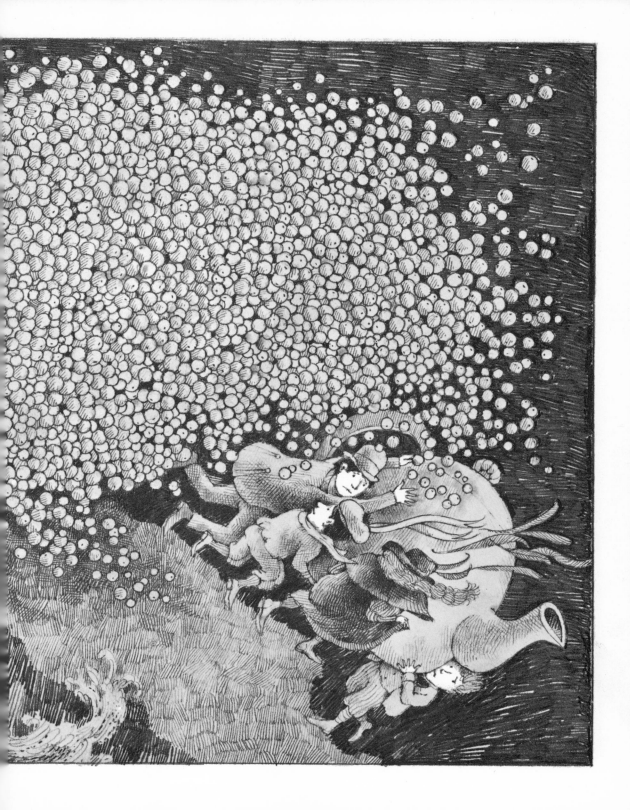

Nevertheless they got safely to the boat, although considerably vexed and hurt; and the Quangle-Wangle's right foot was so knocked about that he had to sit with his head in his slipper for at least a week.

This event made them all for a time rather melancholy: and perhaps they might never have become less so had not Lionel, with a most praiseworthy devotion and perseverance, continued to stand on one leg and whistle to them in a loud and lively manner; which diverted the whole party so extremely that they gradually recovered their spirits and agreed that whenever they should reach home they would subscribe toward a testimonial to Lionel, entirely made of gingerbread and raspberries, as an earnest token of their sincere and grateful infection.

14

After sailing on calmly for several more days they came to another country, where they were much pleased and surprised to see a countless multitude of white Mice with red eyes all sitting in a great circle, slowly eating custard pudding with the most satisfactory and polite demeanor.

15

And as the four travelers were rather hungry, being tired of eating nothing but soles and oranges for so long a period, they held a council as to the propriety of asking the Mice for some of their pudding in a humble and affecting manner, by which they could hardly be otherwise than gratified. It was agreed, therefore, that Guy should go and ask the Mice, which he immediately did; and the result was that they gave him a walnut shell only half full of custard diluted with water. Now this displeased Guy, who said, "Out of

16

such a lot of pudding as you have got, I must say, you might have spared a somewhat larger quantity." But no sooner had he finished speaking than the Mice turned round at once and sneezed at him in an appalling and vindictive manner (and it is impossible to imagine a more scroobious and unpleasant sound than that caused by the simultaneous sneezing of many millions of angry Mice); so that Guy rushed back to the boat, having first shied his cap into the middle of the custard pudding, by which means he completely spoiled the Mice's dinner.

17

By and by the four children came to a country where there were no houses, but only an incredibly innumerable number of large bottles without corks and of a dazzling and sweetly susceptible blue color. Each of these blue bottles contained a Bluebottle Fly; and all these interesting animals live continually together in the most copious and rural harmony: nor perhaps in many parts of the world is such perfect and abject happiness to be found.

19

Violet and Slingsby and Guy and Lionel were greatly struck with this singular and instructive settlement; and, having previously asked permission of the Bluebottle Flies (which was most courteously granted), the boat was drawn up to the shore and they proceeded to make tea in front of the bottles: but as they had no tea leaves they merely placed some pebbles in the hot water and the Quangle-Wangle played some tunes over it on an accordion, by which, of course, tea was made directly, and of the very best quality.

The four children then entered into conversation with the Bluebottle Flies, who discoursed in a placid and genteel manner though with a slightly buzzing accent, chiefly owing to the fact that they each held a small clothesbrush between their teeth, which naturally occasioned a fizzy, extraneous utterance.

"Why," said Violet, "would you kindly inform us, do you reside in bottles; and, if in bottles at all, why not, rather, in green or purple or, indeed, in yellow bottles?"

To which questions a very aged Bluebottle Fly answered, "We found the bottles here all ready to live in; that is to say, our great-great-great-great-great-grandfathers did: so we occupied them at once. And when the winter comes on we turn the bottles upside down and consequently rarely feel the cold at all; and you know very well that this could not be the case with bottles of any other color than blue."

20

"Of course it could not," said Slingsby. "But, if we may take the liberty of inquiring, on what do you chiefly subsist?"

"Mainly on oyster patties," said the Bluebottle Fly, "and when these are scarce on raspberry vinegar and Russian leather boiled down to a jelly."

"How delicious!" said Guy.

To which Lionel added, "Huzz!" And all the Bluebottle Flies said, "Buzz!"

At this time an elderly Fly said it was the hour for the evening song to be sung; and, on a signal being given, all the Bluebottle Flies began to buzz at once in a sumptuous and sonorous manner, the melodious and mucilaginous sounds echoing all over the waters and resounding across the tumultuous tops of the transitory titmice upon the inter- vening and verdant mountains with a serene and sickly suavity only known to the truly virtuous. The Moon was shining slobaciously from the star-bespangled sky, while her light irrigated the smooth and shiny sides and wings and backs of the Bluebottle Flies with a peculiar and trivial splendor, while all Nature cheerfully responded to the cerulean and conspicuous circumstances.

In many long-after years, the four little travelers looked back to that evening as one of the happiest in all their lives; and it was already past midnight when—the sail of the boat having been set up by the Quangle-Wangle, the teakettle and churn placed in their respective positions and the Pussy Cat stationed at the helm—the children each took a last and affectionate farewell of the Bluebottle Flies, who walked down in a body to the water's edge to see the travelers embark.

As a token of parting respect and esteem Violet made a courtesy quite down to the ground and stuck one of her few remaining parrot tail feathers into the back hair of the most pleasing of the Bluebottle Flies; while Slingsby, Guy and Lionel offered them three small boxes containing, respectively, black pins, dried figs and Epsom salts; and thus they left that happy shore forever.

Overcome by their feelings, the four little travelers instantly jumped into the teakettle and fell fast asleep. But all along the shore, for many hours, there was distinctly heard a sound of severely suppressed sobs and of a vague multitude of living creatures using their pocket handkerchiefs in a subdued simultaneous snuffle, lingering sadly along the walloping waves as the boat sailed farther and farther away from the Land of the Happy Bluebottle Flies.

Nothing particular occurred for some days after these events except that as the travelers were passing a low tract of sand they perceived an unusual and gratifying spectacle; namely, a large number of Crabs and Crawfish—perhaps six or seven hundred—sitting by the waterside and endeavoring to disentangle a vast heap of pale pink worsted, which they moistened at intervals with a fluid composed of lavender water and white wine negus.

"Can we be of any service to you, O crusty Crabbies?" said the four children.

"Thank you kindly," said the Crabs consecutively. "We are trying to make some worsted mittens but do not know how."

On which Violet, who was perfectly acquainted with the art of mitten-making, said to the Crabs, "Do your claws unscrew or are they fixtures?"

"They are all made to unscrew," said the Crabs, and forthwith they deposited a great pile of claws close to the boat, with which Violet uncombed all the pale pink worsted and then made the loveliest mittens with it you can imagine. These the Crabs, having resumed and screwed on their claws, placed cheerfully upon their wrists, and walked away rapidly on their hind legs warbling songs with a silvery voice and in a minor key.

After this the four little people sailed on again till they came to a vast and wide plain of astonishing dimensions on which nothing whatever could be discovered at first; but as the travelers walked onward there appeared in the extreme and dim distance a single object, which on a nearer approach and on an accurately cutaneous inspection seemed to be somebody in a large white wig, sitting on an armchair made of spongecakes and oyster shells.

"It does not quite look like a human being," said Violet doubtfully; nor could they make out what it really was till the Quangle-Wangle (who had previously been round the world) exclaimed softly in a loud voice, "It is the cooperative Cauliflower!"

And so in truth it was: and they soon found that what they had taken for an immense wig was in reality the top of the Cauliflower; and that he had no feet at all, being able to walk tolerably well with a fluctuating and graceful movement on a single cabbage stalk—an accomplishment which naturally saved him the expense of stockings and shoes.

Presently, while the whole party from the boat was gazing at him with mingled affection and disgust, he suddenly arose and, in a somewhat plumdomphious manner, hurried off toward the setting sun—his steps supported by two superincumbent confidential Cucumbers, and a large number of Water Wagtails proceeding in advance of him by three and three in a row—till he finally disappeared on the brink of the western sky in a crystal cloud of sudorific sand.

So remarkable a sight of course impressed the four children very deeply and they returned immediately to their boat with a strong sense of undeveloped asthma and a great appetite.

Shortly after this the travelers were obliged to sail directly below some high overhanging rocks from the top of one of which a particularly odious little boy, dressed in rose-colored knickerbockers and with a pewter plate upon his head, threw an enormous pumpkin at the boat, by which it was instantly upset.

But this upsetting was of no consequence, because all the party knew how to swim very well: and in fact they preferred swimming about till after the Moon rose; when, the water growing chilly, they sponge-taneously entered the boat. Meanwhile the Quangle-Wangle threw back the pumpkin with immense force so that it hit the rocks where the malicious little boy in rose-colored knickerbockers was sitting; when, being quite full of lucifer matches, the pumpkin exploded surreptitiously into a thousand bits; whereon the rocks instantly took fire and the odious little boy became unpleasantly hotter and hotter and hotter, till his knickerbockers were turned quite green and his nose was burnt off.

Two or three days after this had happened they came to another place, where they found nothing at all except some wide and deep pits full of mulberry jam. This is the property of the tiny yellow-nosed Apes who abound in these districts and who store up the mulberry jam for their food in winter, when they mix it with pellucid pale periwinkle soup and serve it out in Wedgwood china bowls, which grow freely all over that part of the country. Only one of the yellow-nosed Apes was on the spot, and he was fast asleep; yet the four travelers and the Quangle-Wangle and Pussy were so terrified by the violence and sanguinary sound of his snoring that they merely took a small cupful of the jam and returned to re-embark in their boat without delay.

What was their horror on seeing the boat (including the churn and the teakettle) in the mouth of an enormous Seeze Pyder, an aquatic and ferocious creature truly dreadful to behold and, happily, only met with in those excessive longi-

tudes! In a moment the beautiful boat was bitten into fifty-five thousand million hundred billion bits, and it instantly became quite clear that Violet, Slingsby, Guy and Lionel could no longer preliminate their voyage by sea.

The four travelers were therefore obliged to resolve on pursuing their wanderings by land: and very fortunately there happened to pass by at that moment an elderly Rhinoceros, on which they seized; and, all four mounting on his back— the Quangle-Wangle sitting on his horn and holding on by his ears and the Pussy Cat swinging at the end of his tail— they set off, having only four small beans and three pounds of mashed potatoes to last through their whole journey.

They were, however, able to catch numbers of the chickens and turkeys and other birds who incessantly alighted on the head of the Rhinoceros for the purpose of gathering the seeds of the rhododendron plants which grew there; and these creatues they cooked in the most translucent and satisfactory manner by means of a fire lighted on the end of the Rhinoceros's back. A crowd of Kangaroos and gigantic Cranes accompanied them, from feelings of curiosity and complacency; so that they were never at a loss for company and went onward, as it were, in a sort of profuse and triumphant procession.

Thus in less than eighteen weeks they all arrived safely at home, where they were received by their admiring relatives with joy tempered with contempt, and where they finally resolved to carry out the rest of their traveling plans at some more favorable opportunity.

As for the Rhinoceros, in token of their grateful adherence, they had him killed and stuffed directly and then set him up outside the door of their father's house as a diaphanous door scraper.

A16002 047722

JF   L So. Amherst gr.4-7   c.3

    Lear, Edward
        The four little children
who went around the world.

OCT 1 0 1970	OCT 2 2 1975
OCT 2 8 1970	NOV 3 1975
DEC 8 1970	DEC 1 7 1975
FEB 8 1971	NOV 2 6 1980
FEB 2 6 1971	FEB - 2 1981
SEP 1 6 1971	NOV 4 - 1982
OCT 9 - 1971	
JAN 2 7 1972	
	JAN 2 8 1992
JUL 1 7 1972	SEP 0 2 1999
AUG 2 2 1972	
JAN 3 0 1973	
GAYLORD	PRINTED IN U.S.A.